PEOPLE SHARE

words by LISA WHEELER

A atheneum ATHENEUM BOOKS FOR YOUNG READERS

WITH PEOPLE

art by MOLLY IDLE

NEW YORK   LONDON   TORONTO   SYDNEY   NEW DELHI

It's good to share a blanket.
It's nice to share some fries.

It's great to share your crayons
BEFORE somebody cries.

It's good to share a window.

It's fun to share a ball.

It's best to share a cupcake
BEFORE you eat it all!

'CAUSE . . .

PEOPLE SHARE WITH PEOPLE!

You grumble, but it's true.
What's yours is yours,
what's mine is mine,
but I'll share mine
with you!

Siblings share
a lot of things—
a room,
a toy,
a pet.

When you're
together all
the time,
you're bound to
get upset!

But it's not just our stuff we share; it's friends and family, too.

Your mom is NOT a wishbone. You can't split her in two!

Oh . . .

People share with people.
There's no need to fight!
What's yours is yours,
what's mine is mine,

but we can be polite.

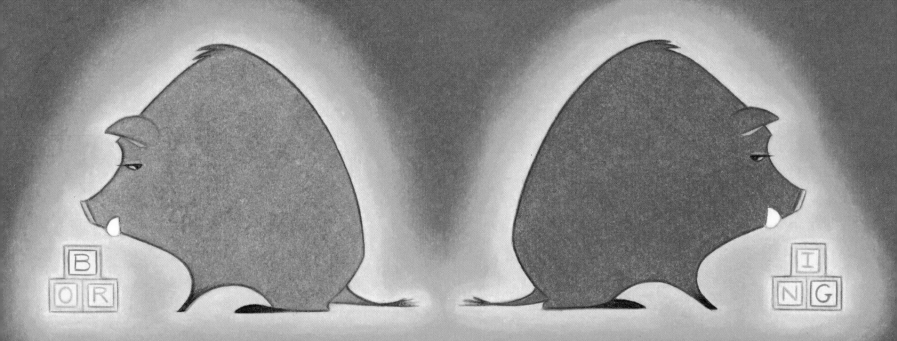

Boars and crocs don't share their toys.

These beasts live in the wild.

You're **NOT** a savage animal.

You **ARE** a human child.

So when your friends come by to play,
don't hoard or hide your loot.
Quit the gruff and share your stuff.
Selfish isn't cute!

People share with people.
We DON'T live in a zoo!
What's yours is yours,
what's mine is mine—

I CHOOSE
to share
with you.

Someone has a yellow car.
You decide to grab it.

But they're not done, and it's no fun
when you just up and nab it!

Slow down, dude! No need to rush;
let's try communication.
First say "please," then wait your turn.
That's called COOPERATION!

Say it with me!

People share with people.
So what if there's just one?
What's yours is yours,
what's mine is mine—

I'll share when
I am done.

There ARE some things
we SHOULDN'T share:
a toothbrush, cup, or hat.
And please, oh PLEASE,
don't share your sneeze!
I hope you all know that!

Instead,
why not share
bigger things
like

LOVE,

RES

PECT,

and TIME.

This great big world
is OURS to share.

It's AWESOME to be kind!

Yes, people share
with people.

So if you see
a frown . . .

show your style

and SHARE a smile . . .

They make
the world
go round!

For Oliver, who had
to share from the
beginning
—L. W.

For John and Tom, who
share a room, a mom, a
dad, and all my love
—M. I.